SEA HORSE, RUN!

Bookaroos®
Publishing, Inc.
Fayetteville, AR

Tammy
Carter
Bronson

Bookaroos® Publishing, Inc.
P. O. Box 8518
Fayetteville, AR 72703 USA
www.bookaroos.com
books@bookaroos.com

First Printing, 2011
Printed in the United States of America.

Publisher's Cataloging-in-Publication
(Provided by Quality Books, Inc.)

Bronson, Tammy Carter.
    Sea Horse, run! / text and illustrations by Tammy
Carter Bronson.
    p. cm.
    SUMMARY: Rumors of an approaching sea dragon cause
frightened sea creatures to flee the reef, but brave Sea
Horse stays behind to defend his helpless friend, Coral.
    Audience: Ages 3-10.
    LCCN 2010913234
    ISBN-13: 978-0-9678167-7-7
    ISBN-10: 0-9678167-7-7
    ISBN-13: 978-0-9678167-8-4
    ISBN-10: 0-9678167-8-5

    1. Sea horses--Juvenile fiction. 2. Coral reefs and
islands--Juvenile fiction. 3. Sea dragons--Juvenile
fiction. 4. Courage--Juvenile fiction. 5. Friendship--
Juvenile fiction. [1. Sea horses--Fiction. 2. Coral
reefs and islands--Fiction. 3. Sea dragons--Fiction.
4. Courage--Fiction. 5. Friendship--Fiction.] I. Title.

PZ7.B7893Sea 2011   [E]
            QBI10-600214

For anyone

willing to find

courage

in the face

of adversity.

Far across the ocean a reef kissed the surface of
the water. Coral covered the reef, and Coral was alive.
Coral loved to sing, but the only animal that could
hear her song was Sea Horse.

Sea Horse could swim, but Coral could not. Coral was rooted in the rock. When the current was strong, Sea Horse clung to Coral with his tail.

 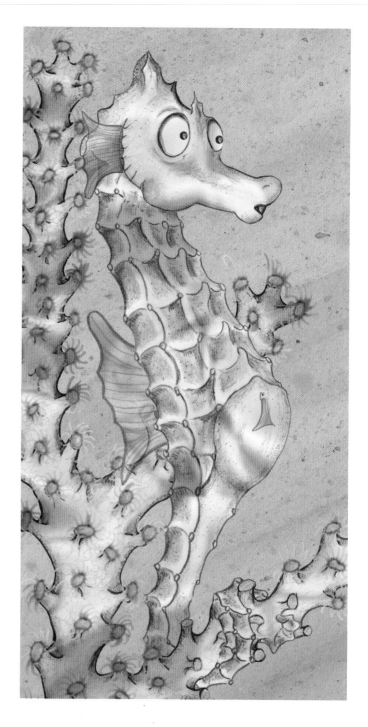

When Coral was red,
Sea Horse looked red.

When Coral was yellow,
Sea Horse turned yellow.

When Sea Horse was
not with Coral, he was
blue like the sea.

One day several sharks darted past the reef. When one shark veered too close, Coral sang,

"Sea Horse, run far, far away."

Sea Horse hugged Coral and said, "Stop, Shark! Why do you flee?"

Shark trembled from the tip of his nose to the end of his tail. "A sea dragon is coming. Sea dragons are fearsome, terrible beasts. They have ten rows of teeth that chomp sharks into bits. Sea Horse, run!" With a swoosh of his tail Shark plunged into the wide, dark sea.

"Silly shark," said Sea Horse. "He has more rows of teeth than a sea dragon."

A moray eel slithered out of her cave and rippled toward them. Coral sang,

"Sea Horse, run far, far away."

Sea Horse refused to abandon Coral. As Eel slipped by, Sea Horse asked, "Have you seen a dragon?"

Eel replied, "No, but Octopus said a dragon's jaws can snap a whale in two. Sea Dragon gobbles sharks for dinner and slurps eels for dessert. He will eat you, too. Sea Horse, run!"

Now Sea Horse was worried. Should he swim away?

Above them, eight slimy legs unfurled. Coral sang,

"Sea Horse, run far, far away."

Sea Horse did not budge. He curled his tail around Coral and asked Octopus, "Are you running away, too?"

"Running?" Octopus fixed a bulbous eye on Sea Horse. "I am swimming. I plan to follow Shark and Eel. Sea Dragon's tentacles will engulf the entire reef. His scales are very sharp."

"Sharp enough to hurt Coral?"

"Sharp enough to crunch Coral." Octopus whooshed away in a cloud of ink whispering, "Sea Horse, swim!"

Sea Horse was puzzled. "Sharks swim far and wide, eels slither into dark places, and octopi are clever. If they are afraid, we should be, too."

Coral trilled, "I am afraid for you."

Sea Horse said, "I can swim away, but you cannot. I will protect you, Coral. I will save you from the dragon!"

Coral chanted, "Sea Horse, run! Sea Horse, run! Sea Horse, run! "

Sea Horse did not run. He hid behind the giant clam and gazed into the vast, blue ocean beyond the reef. Sea Horse watched and waited, waited and watched, but he did not see a dragon.

Far in the distance he spied a weed floating in the current. "Seaweed," he cried, "float this way!" Sea Horse swam out to meet the plant.

Slowly the seaweed drifted toward Sea Horse. When it was near enough, Sea Horse hooked his tail around a leaf and said, "Come with me, Seaweed. I will help you hide."

Seaweed asked, "What am I hiding from?"

"Sea Dragon. But do not be afraid. You are safe on the reef. I am here to protect you."

Seaweed chuckled. "Brave little Sea Horse! What am I?"

Sea Horse replied, "You are a helpless weed in need of my protection."

"You are wrong. Have you ever met a plant with two eyes and a snout? Look closely. Are you sure I am a weed?"

Sea Horse inspected every leaf as Coral sang,

"I see, I see!"

Sea Horse turned red. "I do not see. I cannot

find two eyes, and

I do not see

a snout."

Finally, Sea Horse found a face. "You look like me! Is this a trick? What are you?"

"I am a sea dragon."

Sea Horse laughed. "You are not a dragon! Dragons are monstrous, terrible beasts with fifty rows of teeth. Dragons gobble whales for dinner and slurp giant squid for dessert. You are a weed with two eyes and a snout. How could you be a sea dragon?"

"Dear little Sea Horse, do you believe everything that you hear? Truly I am a dragon, and I am here to visit another dragon."

Sea Horse was amazed. "A sea dragon lives on the reef?"

"Of course! There he is. That is my cousin, Ribbon."

A slim, green fish wiggled out of the sea grass. Ribbon exclaimed, "Hello, Leafy!"

"Hello, Ribbon!" Leafy hugged Coral with his delicate tail. Coral blushed red. Leafy Dragon turned red, too.

Sea Horse smiled. He was related to dragons.

When Shark and Eel and Octopus returned, Leafy Dragon looked nervous. What if Octopus crushed them in her tentacles? What if Eel bit them in half? What if Shark swallowed them whole?

Sea Horse said, "Do not worry, Leafy Dragon. They cannot see you. You look like a weed."

Ribbon piped up, "We have another cousin named 'Weedy.'"

Coral sang, "Three little dragons! Three little dragons!"

Sea Horse smiled. Maybe he would meet Weedy Dragon, too.

THE END

SEA HORSES

Sea horses are classified in the family **Syngnathidae** (pronounced sin-NATH-ih-dee). Every animal in this family is a fish. Syngnathdae is Greek for 'fused jaws' because the mouths of fish in this family do not open or close. About 330 species of Syngnathidae have been classified. Thirty-seven of these species are sea horses, three are sea dragons, and the rest are pipehorses or pipefishes.

Where do sea horses live?
Most sea horses live in shallow ocean water near land. Sea horses may be found in estuaries, mangrove swamps, sea grass meadows, or reefs around the world.

Why do sea horses hide?
Larger fish like tuna or red snapper eat sea horses. Sea turtles, sting rays, sharks and even penguins munch on sea horses, too. Sea horses hide from these predators by changing color to match their environment.

How do sea horses move?
Sea horses move slowly by means of fins that beat as fast as 70 times per second! The **dorsal fin** propels the sea horse forwards. The two, small **pectoral fins** behind the **gills** allow the sea horse to hover or change direction.

What do sea horses eat?
Sea horses do not have teeth, so they swallow their food whole. Sea horses suck food into their long, narrow **snout**, but the food must be tiny to fit through their mouth. Sea horses eat zooplankton, little shrimp, and the larvae of fish, crab, or worms. Sea horses do not have stomachs either. Without a stomach, sea horses cannot digest food well, so they have to eat large amounts in order to survive. Sea horses may eat for up to 10 hours per day, and they may swallow 50 to 300 tiny animals per hour!

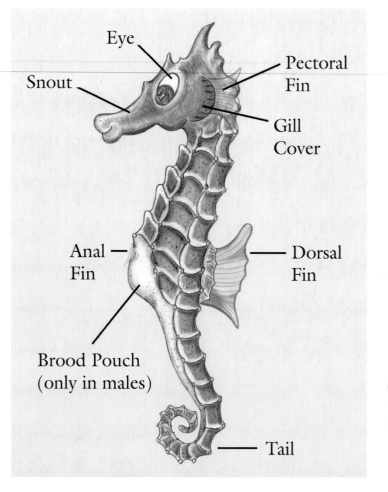

Eye

Snout

Pectoral Fin

Gill Cover

Anal Fin

Dorsal Fin

Brood Pouch (only in males)

Tail

What is the largest sea horse?
The Big-Bellied Sea Horse (*Hippocampus abdominalis*) is the largest species. These sea horses may reach fourteen inches in length which is two inches taller than this book!

What is the smallest sea horse?
Hippocampus denise is a pygmy sea horse that measures about half an inch in length.

LIFE CYCLE OF A SEA HORSE

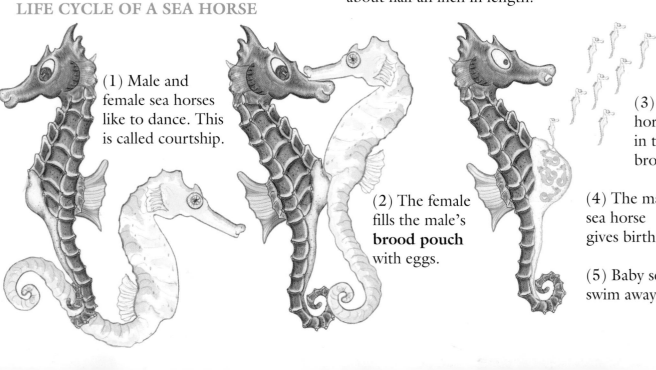

(1) Male and female sea horses like to dance. This is called courtship.

(2) The female fills the male's **brood pouch** with eggs.

(3) Baby sea horses grow in the male's brood pouch.

(4) The male sea horse gives birth!

(5) Baby sea horses swim away.

Sea dragons are among the slowest fish in the ocean. Since they move at a snail's pace, sea dragons rely completely on camouflage to escape predators. Sea dragons have delicate branches of skin that mimic seaweed, and a healthy sea dragon may change color and blend with its surroundings. Leafy sea dragons live in kelp forests along the southern coast of Australia. Leafy sea dragons found in shallow water are yellow or green. In deep water 'leafies' turn red. The colors of ribboned sea dragons are similar to leafies, but they are found in waters northwest of Australia. Weedy sea dragons are easier to find along Australia's southern coast, but their color and leafy appendages vary depending on the environment. Female sea dragons give their eggs to the male who will carry the eggs under his tail until they hatch.

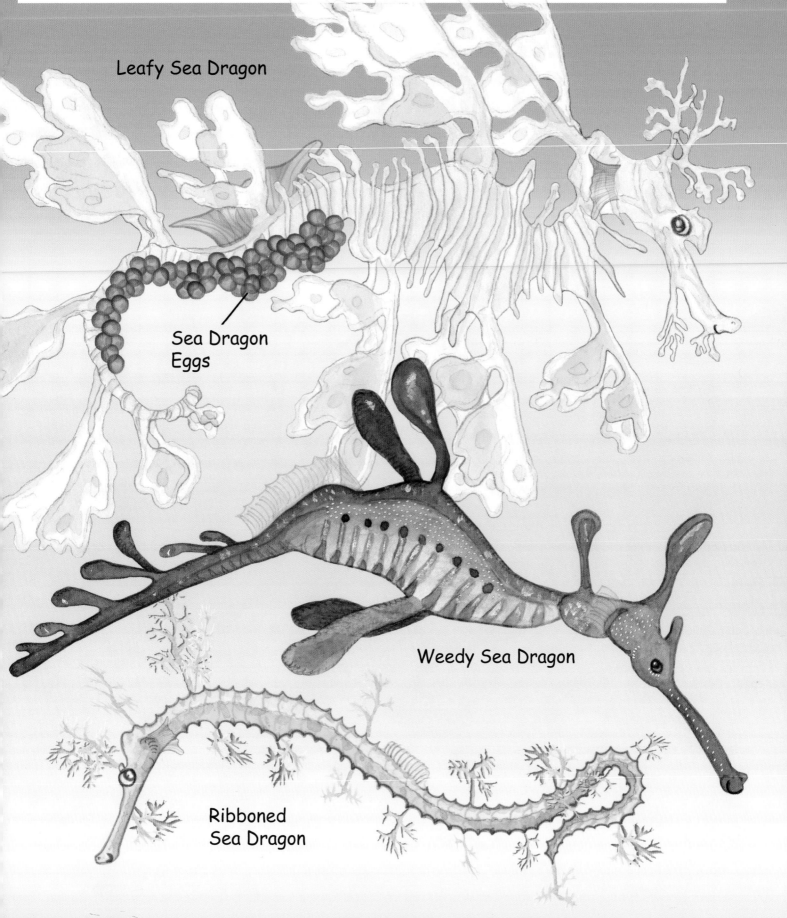

Leafy Sea Dragon

Sea Dragon
Eggs

Weedy Sea Dragon

Ribboned
Sea Dragon

ANIMALS OF THE AUSTRALIAN CORAL REEF

Violet Snail

Blacktip Reef Shark

Jellyfish

Staghorn Coral

Sea Whip Coral

Pearl Perch

Fire Coral

Sea Anemone

Moorish Idol Fish

Sea Fan Coral

Clown Fish

Moray Eel

Fan Worm

Sea Pen Coral

Frog Fish

Thorny Black Coral

Blue Coral

Soft Tree Coral

Bubble Coral

Common Gurnard Perch

Brain Coral

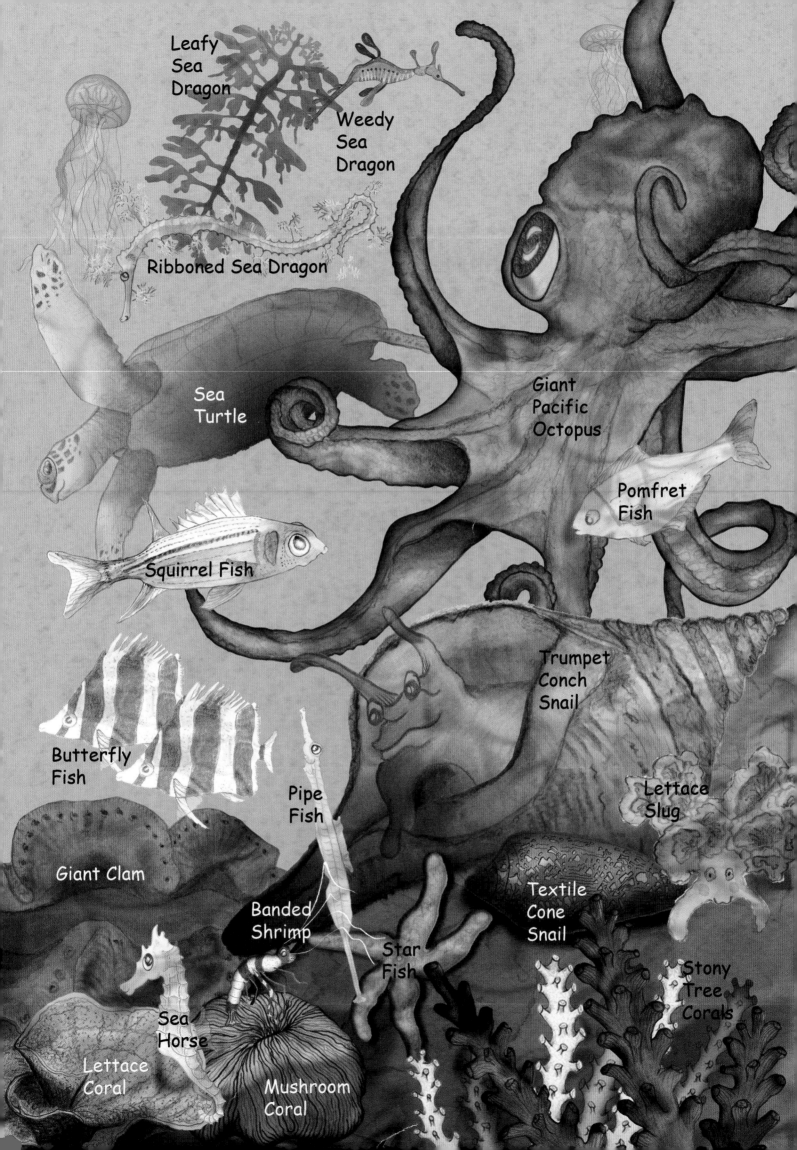

CORAL

Why did Sea Horse's friend, Coral, sing in the story?

In the English language the words 'coral' (c-o-r-a-l) and 'choral' (c-h-o-r-a-l) share the same pronunciation. A coral (c-o-r-a-l) is a colony or group of many polyps. The word 'choral' (c-h-o-r-a-l) generally describes the music sung by a chorus or choir. Each coral on the reef has many polyps, so if a coral living on the reef could talk, it would have many voices speaking as one just like a chorus!

CORAL REEFS

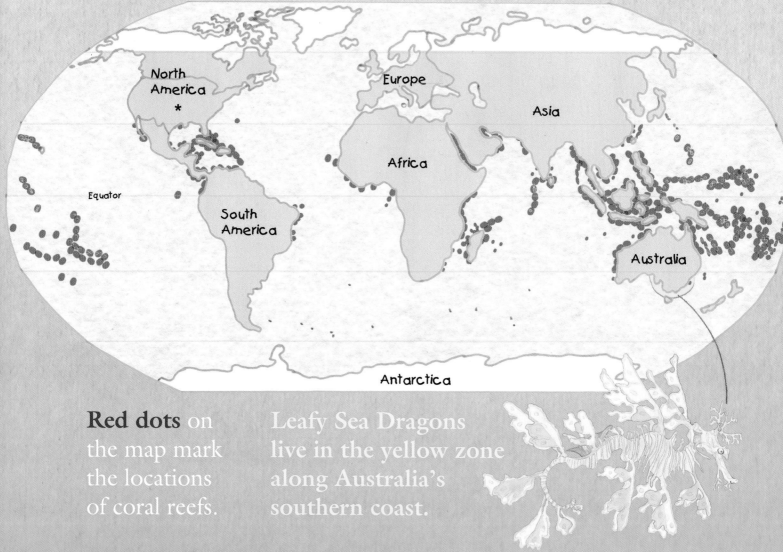

Red dots on the map mark the locations of coral reefs.

Leafy Sea Dragons live in the yellow zone along Australia's southern coast.

ABOUT THE AUTHOR/ILLUSTRATOR

*Tammy Carter Bronson is the author and illustrator of *Tiny Snail*, *Polliwog*, and *The Kaleidonotes & the Mixed-Up Orchestra*. *Sea Horse, run!* is her fourth picture book. Tammy lives in Fayetteville, Arkansas in the middle of the United States. What does a landlocked mammal like Tammy have in common with fish living on the other side of the world? Tammy and the leafy sea dragons live in opposite hemispheres at about the same latitude (36 degrees). That means when it is winter in Arkansas it is summer at Kangaroo Island, but no matter what time of year it is, both Tammy and the leafies move at a snail's pace.

Visit www.seahorserun.com for fun facts, activities, and more!